A Youth's Look
at **Black & Brown Faces**
in **America's Wild Places**

Dudley Edmondson

Adventure Publications, Inc.
Cambridge, Minnesota

Preface

So what do you want to be when you grow up? Have you ever thought about working in the outdoors? You could travel around the world discovering new plants and animals in the jungles as a biologist. Or imagine being a park ranger and helping people enjoy their visit to Grand Canyon National Park, teaching them how the canyon was formed and what plants and animals live there. What if you could ride your bike to work every day? You might be able to do just that if you worked as a camp counselor, teaching kids how to paddle canoes, set up tents, or how to build a campfire.

Perhaps, like me, you have had friends tease you about loving nature and the outdoors. Don't let others determine your future—plot your own course! Your life is an open book full of blank pages. It is up to you fill those pages with interesting and fun things. Working in the outdoors and experiencing nature can fill your life's book with adventures, while teaching you about the creatures who share this earth.

Some African American kids think that the outdoors is 'for white kids' only, and that is simply not true. Consider your African roots, and the close connection your ancestors had to the outdoors, living with and understanding the plants and animals around them. This proud natural heritage is a part of who you are and who you will be.

There are so many job opportunities out there for you in outdoor fields! A job is more than about making a lot of money. A job should also be something you enjoy and are proud to do each and every day. Choose a job you love.

Many kids today want to be professional athletes, singers or movie stars, but these are very, very difficult jobs to get. If that does not work out for you, do you have a backup plan?

Take a look at what the people in this booklet do for a living. Many of them might remind you of your parents or other relatives, people you know and love. Listen to what they have to say about working in and enjoying the outdoors, and then make up your own mind. You can be whatever you want to be—don't let anyone tell you anything different. Explore the possibilities and don't limit yourself.

Whether or not you choose to work in it, nature is out there for you. No matter where you live, you can find a bit of the outdoors, often as close your own backyard—check it out and you may even learn something new about yourself.

Booklet design by Jonathan Norberg
Photo on page 42 copyright by Nancy Latour-Edmondson
All other photos copyright by Dudley Edmondson

Copyright 2006 by Dudley Edmondson
Published by Adventure Publications, Inc.
820 Cleveland St. S
Cambridge, MN 55008
1-800-678-7006
www.adventurepublications.net
All rights reserved
Printed in China
ISBN-10: 1-59193-175-4
ISBN-13: 978-1-59193-175-1

About This Booklet

This booklet is sold as part of a set with the larger book, *The Black & Brown Faces in America's Wild Places* (ISBN-13: 978-159193-173-7), also by Dudley Edmondson. It is also available separately (ISBN-13: 978-159193-175-1).

About Watchable Wildlife

Watchable Wildlife, Inc. has a simple mission:

"To Help Communities and Wildlife Prosper"

We work toward this mission in three key areas: publications like this book and our wildlife viewing guides, our annual conference, and on-the-ground projects. We work primarily with our federal and state partners, community leaders, and wildlife professionals. We work to address the growing list of challenges these agencies and wildlife professionals face in their attempts to protect our wildlife and natural areas.

Watchable Wildlife, Inc. wishes to thank all of our partners who helped us with this important work. We especially want to thank the National Wildlife Refuge System, the U.S. Fish and Wildlife Service, and the Department of the Interior for their help arranging interviews for this publication project.

Shelton Johnson

Interpretive Ranger, Yosemite National Park and Buffalo Soldier Historian
El Portal, California

What I Do in the Outdoors

Afternoon folks, my name is Elizy Boman, and I'm a soldier with the 9th Calvary of the U.S. Army. Natives call us Buffalo Soldiers, and I've been assigned to these here parts by the U.S. government to keep folks from misusing these federally protected lands. My regiment rode for 14 days from San Francisco at the Presidio to get here. I tell ya, it's nice duty if you can get it. The air here is so cool and fresh, and timber so tall just makes a man happy to be alive.

You know you have been talking to a ghost, don't you? Because soldiers like Elizy have not been in the park since 1904. But the important thing is that black soldiers like him were here protecting the park before the Park Service was in existence. I am a park ranger here in Yosemite National Park, and I interpret the park's natural and cultural history through the soldier character Elizy Boman, doing my naturalist program in full Spanish-American War period uniform. Buffalo Soldiers were here in the park in 1899, 1903 and 1904. Many people only know of Buffalo Soldiers' participation in the Indian wars, but few know about their role in protecting some of our national parks.

A typical day for me would be working at the Valley visitor center, getting people oriented to what things are available to them while they are in the park. These include canoe trips, hiking trails or going on a ranger-led tram tour of the park. I give botany, wildlife and cultural history talks and walks. I have been doing that here in Yosemite for about 12 years. I have actually been a park ranger for about 19 years. It is a great experience to see someone's eyes light up about an aspect of Yosemite's natural or cultural history.

I tend to think of being a park ranger as a calling, as opposed to an occupation. People don't join the Park Service to make a lot of money. They join it because of some kind of personal belief system about human beings and their role in nature, especially in the preservation of the natural world.

For me being a park ranger is like my childhood dream coming true, having the opportunity to spend my life in the mountains, or in the desert, or wherever I happen to be, just to be in a place where there are not a lot of people but there is a lot of nature around me.

Best Outdoor Experiences and Favorite Places

One of my last jobs when I worked in Yellowstone was to deliver the mail in winter. I did the run twice a week. It was 150 miles by snowmobile, round-trip. I would go out in all kinds of weather because, as you know, "the mail always goes through." I had a chance to experience the park months before the park roads reopened to visitors. So when I was out there, frequently I was all by myself in Yellowstone's 2.2 million acres. I would not see any people most of the time, until I delivered the mail on the other end. There would be huge stretches of wilderness where the only thing I would see were bison. You had a lot of time to contemplate the meaning of wilderness when you are driving through it in the middle of a snowstorm, wondering if you are going to make it. That is another thing about wilderness—nature does have an edge, but it also is an excellent place to learn who you are as a person and your strengths and weaknesses.

For me being a park ranger is like my childhood dream coming true, having the opportunity to spend my life in the mountains, or in the desert, or wherever I happen to be, just to be in a place where there are not a lot of people but there is a lot of nature around me.

Cheryl Armstrong

President and CEO, James P. Beckwourth Mountain Club
Denver, Colorado

What I Do in the Outdoors

The James P. Beckwourth Mountain Club was named after a true legend of the West. Beckwourth was born in 1798 in Fredericksburg County, Virginia, to a white plantation owner and one of his African American female slaves. He was raised in Missouri. Around 23 years of age he joined the Rocky Mountain Fur Trading Company as a hunter, and over his long fascinating life he was, among other things, a frontiersman and an exceptional explorer. He discovered a pass over the Sierra Nevada Mountains that would lead pioneers into the Sacramento Valley of California. He saved the life of General Zachary Taylor, who later became President of the United States. Beckwourth was also war chief of the Crow Indian nation.

The reason we started the Beckwourth Mountain Club (it was formed in 1993) was because of our passion to bring the outdoors to inner city youth. We take urban youth into the outdoors for hiking, fishing, camping, backpacking, snowshoeing, whitewater rafting, canoeing and kayaking. We teach them mapping and compass skills as well as self-arrest training and leadership skills.

The organization is run by a terrific group of almost 60 volunteers, primarily people of color. They act as mentors, chaperones, hike leaders, instructors and historical reenactors. Membership is for families, singles and seniors. We do outdoor activities every single weekend, all the way from easy day hikes, to climbs of Colorado's peaks, to upscale trips such as orca watching on the San Juan Islands off the coast of Washington state, and trips to national parks such as Acadia in Maine, and Yellowstone.

I also do a great deal of fund raising. I am the grant writer and public relations person. I travel around the country heading up panel discussions and workshops, doing presentations on our program. I guess you could say I wear about 15 different hats around here.

I spent many years in the legal profession, but eight years ago I was able to break away and do what I truly love and have a passion for. There is no comparison salary-wise between working for a nonprofit organization and being in the legal profession, but I would not do anything else even if you gave me a million dollars. I enjoy running this organization and doing what we do for the community.

Best Outdoor Experiences and Favorite Places

My favorite outdoor activity is and always has been horseback riding. I have been riding since I was five years old and still love it. Being on the back of a horse on a trail, climbing up into the mountains and wilderness areas of Colorado makes me feel like I am truly at home. Camping out under the stars and seeing the beauty of the constellations with no light pollution from cities puts me in a whole other state of mind. It relaxes me and takes away all the stress that I may have had. Nothing makes me feel the same way; nothing is even comparable.

Some of my more memorable experiences in the outdoors with my father and my family include touring the ruins of the fabulous city Angkor Wat in Cambodia, and climbing the pyramids in the ruins of the ancient Mayan city, Chichen Itza, on the Yucatan Peninsula in Mexico. We rode camels at sunset in the desert in Algiers, Morocco; it was just beautiful. We rode elephants while in Thailand and Cambodia. My father enjoyed life and enjoyed world travel, and he has given me outdoor experiences I will never forget. I feel very fortunate.

Here in the United States, some of my more memorable experiences include seeing the Grand Canyon at sunrise. And seeing a female grizzly with her cubs and, on the same morning, a wolf pack in the Lamar Valley of Yellowstone National Park. In New Mexico I took a night at the cliff dwelling of Bandolier National Monument. We saw thousands and thousands of bats emerging from their caves at dusk.

But my favorite place to spend time outdoors is in Colorado's Rocky Mountain National Park. I say that even though I have traveled all over the world and seen some pretty incredible places. I have been in just about every state in this country, but for me nothing can compare with the beauty of Rocky Mountain National Park.

My favorite outdoor activity is and always has been horseback riding.

Bill Gwaltney

Assistant Regional Director of Workforce Enhancement, National Park Service
Denver, Colorado

What I Do in the Outdoors

I grew up in Washington, D.C. I was always interested in the West—its landscape, its peoples, its history. I was driven, in part, like so many eight-year-old kids, by my interest in the Native American culture. Like a lot of African Americans, my family has Indian ancestry, both the Pamonkey people in Virginia and some of the New England tribes on my mom's side.

My grandfather noticed I had a real thing for John Wayne westerns. So after weeks of this, he came to me one day and said, "You know, when you get done with that John Wayne western, I got some vanilla ice cream in the kitchen for you." Of course, that really focused my eight-year-old attention. Over a bowl of Breyer's vanilla ice cream, my grandfather told me what he knew of African Americans as soldiers, as pioneers, and as trappers in the West. I almost immediately lost interest in those John Wayne westerns. The Saturdays I spent with him after that, for years, were spent at the Library of Congress and at the National Archives, trying to find images of African Americans in the West. We did not find a lot of images, but we found enough. This then gave me the sense, both intellectually and emotionally, that if I wanted to do things western, and if I wanted to live in the West, there was a historical precedence for it. So that led me to history, and, in many regards, history led me to the Park Service.

After 26 years of working for the Park Service, I find myself as an assistant regional director, in a very singular job which attempts to find ways to bring people of color into the parks both as visitors and as employees of the National Park Service workforce. In many regards, the faces of America are not reflected in our workforce at present, and have not been in the past.

In my career I have done a lot of different jobs for the Park Service. I started in my hometown of Washington, D.C., at the National Mall, where I worked at the Lincoln Memorial. I am proud to say my career in the outdoors spans over 30 years. I have been a park ranger, a law enforcement officer and a wild land firefighter. I have been involved in Park Service search and rescue activities—pretty much the full range of ranger stuff. I was also Chief of Interpretation at Rocky Mountain National Park. I was the first African American to hold a position like that in that park.

Best Outdoor Experiences and Favorite Places

I can remember sleeping under a larch tree and I have never felt so rested when I awoke; the best bed I have ever been in was under that tree. The taste of trout stuffed with wild meat and stories around hunting camps. Being alone in the wilderness with the sound of your horse's hooves along a rocky trail echoing all around you. Water so cold it hurts to drink it. Camping out and waking up in a tent that is covered with a foot and a half of snow. These are things that drive so deeply to the core of who you are as a human being, words really don't suffice. I think they all change your life for the better, because they make you a better person, a more prepared person and a more connected person.

I have been a park ranger, a law enforcement officer and a wild land firefighter. I have been involved in Park Service search and rescue activities—pretty much the full range of ranger stuff.

Elliott Boston III

Experienced Mountaineer
Springfield, Missouri

What I Do in the Outdoors

I am trying to become the first African American to summit the seven highest peaks on earth. Each one lies on a different continent. To date, I have successfully done four of them. I have summited the South American peak, Aconcagua, which is the tallest mountain in the western hemisphere, in Argentina, at 22,841 feet. I have climbed the European peak of Mount Elbrus in Russia, at 18,481 feet. On the African continent, I have climbed the highest peak, Mount Kilimanjaro, at 19,339 feet. And finally, the highest Australian peak is Mount Kosciusko, at 7,000 feet, which I have also climbed. To fund my climbs, I solicit sponsors; these have included Volvo, the North Face and Pepsi. I do a lot of it out of pocket, tapping my own savings as well, but I could not do it all without generous sponsors.

In my training to climb high altitude mountains I do a lot of trail running, mountain biking and working out with weights. I do strength training, not the body building stuff. I like to ride my mountain bike for six hours or more along a trail up by St. Louis. This will help me get ready to go for Everest or my climb of Mount Vincent in Antarctica.

My passion for climbing is centered on the challenge it brings. The skills I use during climbing can be applied to everyday life. I may sit there, frustrated, a thousand feet above the ground with a particular climb or route, and say to myself, "I think you need to go back down a bit and think the whole thing through again." I will sit there hanging from the rope for a while and go over it in my mind, looking at my successes and my failures, and go back up to try it again, trying to solve the problems one at a time until I have succeeded.

It is a sport I love. I will always be a climber. I can do it when I am 70 years old. That is one of the things that has always attracted me to doing things outside, that it has no age limitations.

Best Outdoor Experiences and Favorite Places

I was in Uganda in 2000 and Tanzania and Kenya to climb Kilimanjaro in 2003. There is always a connection to Africa. Most of the people are very friendly and many of them speak English. They feel connected to you because they know that a long time ago you, too, had deep ties to that continent and you are part of them. Once you leave the airport and begin to drive, you are overwhelmed with this beautiful, vast, open countryside. In terms of natural resources, it is an extremely rich continent, perhaps the richest soil you will ever see. The rains in Africa are unbelievable, and once the storm passes it is beautiful. The land becomes so green, the trees and shrubs just pop to life afterwards. The green is so vibrant; it just stays in your mind. I look back at pictures I took there, but they pale in comparison to the memories I have of the place. It is one of those places you have to see to believe how beautiful it is.

One of the more memorable experiences I have had was a sea kayaking trip I did in Prince William Sound in Alaska. You could follow the coast, and kayak into Juneau. We saw a few ecotourism vessels showing groups of people glaciers, but other than that we had no human contact for 11 days. We saw all kinds of cool wildlife, like moose, bald eagles, salmon runs and sea otters. We started campfires from scratch, cooked dinner—it was a very memorable journey. The place was absolutely beautiful! Once you have been to a place like Alaska and seen the vastness of the land, you could spend a lifetime exploring it and never see it all.

I am trying to become the first African American to summit the seven highest peaks on earth.

Darryl Perkins

Master Falconer
Boston, Massachusetts

What I Do in the Outdoors

I am the current President of the North American Falconers Association (NAFA). I am fortunate that I am doing exactly what I want to do. I am what I have always wanted to be. I did not want to be a doctor or a lawyer or anything else; I wanted to be a falconer. And the fact that I'm a falconer and a black man and president of the largest falconry organization on earth is beyond my wildest dreams or expectations. We have about 4,000 members in the NAFA organization worldwide. We represent about 40 different countries, and we come from all walks of life. There is no set occupation or socioeconomic status that defines a person being a falconer. It all stems from a love of raptors.

Some folks think that falconry is merely getting a bird and starving it into submission to a point where it has to kill something to live. That is not falconry. There is no starvation in falconry. Most falconers, myself included, try to have their birds be as close to what they would be for weight if they were in the wild. Falconry is the art of hunting using trained raptors.

Best Outdoor Experiences and Favorite Places

Probably the most memorable experience I had in the outdoors was Christmas Day 1989 with my son Jonathan. It was about seven or eight degrees. It was windy with light flurries, and generally nasty out. Jonathan and I decided to go duck hunting on Cape Cod. I was living with a friend at the time, and he had a black lab dog named Kala, and I used to take her duck hunting with me.

I was flying my bird, Lilith, that was a gyrfalcon, prairie and lanner falcon cross, a tri-bred bird. When Kala got to the edge where the marsh opened up, she froze and stopped dead in her tracks. I told my son, "That means the ducks are in there." It was mid tide, and I peeked around there and I saw this large group of black ducks in this little channel.

I stepped back and unhooded the falcon and held her up in the sky, and she took off in typical gyrfalcon fashion. Instead of ringing up, circling up into the sky like a peregrine falcon, she just went up straight away, climbing the whole time like a jet from a runway. When she is about 800 feet up, she comes across the sky over us and the ducks, so now they are pinned down and will not flush because they now know she is up there.

She turns again and this time I lose sight of her. I tell my son, "I lost her, John!" and he says, "Oh, Daddy, I got her, she is just a speck up there! She is right above us." So that was my cue from the falcon to run out into the salt marsh and scream—"Hoo...hooo!"—to flush the ducks. They explode from the water and start flying off. I look up and see Lilith dropping out of the sky. Like a bolt of lightning from the clouds, she strikes a large male black duck, knocking it onto the ice. John said, "Did you hear that, Daddy?" I said, "Oh, yeah! Sounded like a hundred-mile-an-hour fastball popping into a leather glove." Lilith pulled up afterwards like a plane from a nosedive and circled around and headed back towards her downed quarry.

Now the thing I remembered the most about that day was when John said, "I see her, Daddy!" And she started dropping out of the sky, and the ducks were flushing and exploding from the surface of the marsh. For me, for that moment, time just stood still. It was a father, his son, a mongrel dog and a falcon falling out of the sky. Now for me that is what falconry is all about, for me that is what being in the outdoors is all about. It removes all the stresses of daily life.

For me, for that moment, time just stood still. It was a father, his son, a mongrel dog and a falcon falling out of the sky.

Nina Roberts

Educational Outreach Specialist, National Park Service
Fort Collins, Colorado

What I Do in the Outdoors

I work for the National Park Service as an educational outreach specialist. I work for the entire park system, nationwide. I work with teachers across the country in a variety of ways, as well as park staff and park interpretive staff.

I am also in the process of finishing my Ph.D. in natural resource management in parks and protected areas. My primary emphasis is on the human dimension, working with people and their understanding and appreciation of the natural resources, from a quality of life and recreation standpoint.

I have worked in everything from environmental education to adventure-based programs, mostly with high school students. There are fewer and fewer women and girls participating in outdoor activities today than ever before, and there are a lot of myths and stereotypes that exist. So I have also worked with all-girl programs that provide a safe base for young girls to actually enjoy themselves, be free of gender stereotypes, and learn about the benefits of participating in outdoor activities.

Best Outdoor Experiences and Favorite Places

One of the more memorable experiences I have had in the outdoors was touring the country for four months with a friend many years ago in a van. We were free from obligations at the time and had just a little money in our pockets so we just went with it. That trip was saturated with outdoors experiences.

I also had an opportunity to spend some time at the National Outdoor Leadership School, or NOLS. The primary purpose of the course was to continue to help you evolve or develop any outdoor skills you had so that you could be a better leader. The program I was in took place in southwest Arizona, just outside Tucson, in a place called the Galiuros Mountain Range. Everybody had a chance to teach others in the group skills they had an expertise in, so part of the course was to learn from other people.

We spent the month of February in the wilderness, primarily riparian desert environment. That was a new opportunity for me. As much time as I have spent in the outdoors, I had never done anything like that. That is part of why it was so memorable. Most of the time the weather was beautiful, lots of sun and nice temps. One night we camped in a saddle in the mountains. There was a change in the weather patterns that night that none of the four guides had anticipated. It started to snow and it was not letting up. The snowfall got heavier and heavier! So the decision was made in the middle of the night and they woke us up to get prepared to leave the mountains in a rush because we did not have winter gear. This was not a winter camping trip. By the time we were making our way down the mountain we were walking through three to four inches of snow with no winter gear. It was whiteout snow, blowing hard, making it nearly impossible to see where we were going. But aside from that, the month-long adventure was great, with clear blue skies and a lot of fun.

The wilderness and being in the outdoors clears your thinking. That is what I try to teach young people. It provides that relief from stress, it offers mental clarity and just plain relaxation. For me it also provides a certain degree of inner strength. I feel stronger when I come out of the wilderness both physically and mentally, no matter what it is I am doing when I am out there.

There are fewer and fewer women and girls participating in outdoor activities today than ever before, and there are a lot of myths and stereotypes that exist.

Judge Manson retired in late 2005, after the time of this interview.

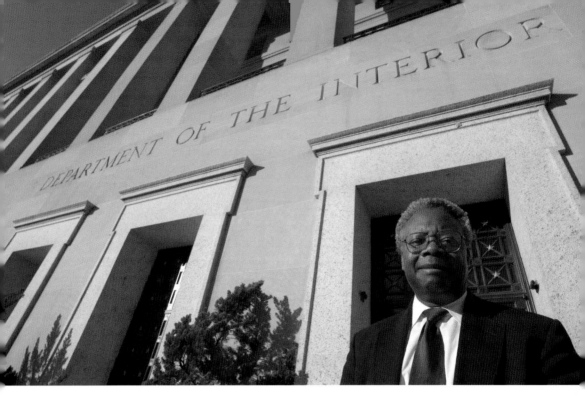

Craig Manson

Assistant Secretary of the Department of the Interior
Washington, D.C.

What I Do in the Outdoors

I am the Assistant Secretary of the Department of the Interior for the U.S. Fish and Wildlife Department and the National Park Service. The directors of those two bureaus report to me. I am responsible to the Secretary of the Interior for seeing that those bureaus function well.

On a typical day, I spend time with the directors of the Park Service and Fish and Wildlife, as well as spending time up on Capitol Hill testifying before Congress or dealing with the budgets of those two bureaus. Also I may have to meet with congressmen who have issues they want to discuss—it seems like every congressman wants a new park in their district or wants one expanded or changed in some fashion.

I find that I enjoy the days out of Washington, D.C., when I get to go out to a park unit and see things on the ground and spend time with the people who are doing what I call the "real work." In the four years that I have been Assistant Secretary, I have been to 47 states and visited several of the 384 national park units and many of the 538 national wildlife refuges I oversee.

Best Outdoor Experiences and Favorite Places

One of my most memorable experiences in the outdoors is one that is both good and bad. A friend of mine is a game warden in Wyoming and he said to me, "Let's take this horse pack trip into the Big Horn Mountains," which is an all-wilderness area; there are no motorized vehicles allowed in at all. I went with him and three other guys from the Wyoming Game and Fish Department. We rode horses into the Big Horns, and there were places along the horse trail where it seemed to be only a few inches wide. I would look down the side of that trail off the mountainside, and there would be a drop-off of hundreds of feet. My instinct, because I do not ride horses that often, was to get off the horse and walk. My friend said, "Look, you have to trust the horse, because first of all the horse does not want to fall off the side of the mountain any more than you do, and secondly the horse knows the trail better than you do!" So I said, "OK, I am going to trust the horse."

We made it into the wilderness, to the site where we were going to camp for six days. Then one night, halfway into our trip, it started to rain while we were fishing about half a mile upstream from where we had camped. We started heading back to camp for shelter and I unfortunately stepped on a wet log and lost my footing. So I slipped and fell and thought I had broken my thigh bone—that is how intense the pain was. I could barely walk as a result. So the only way out was the same way we came in, and that was on horseback. Needless to say, it is pretty difficult to ride a horse when you have only one good leg—the horse wants to keep going around in circles because it does not understand why you are only using one leg.

We rode several miles before we came upon a Forest Service crew that was cutting some timber. The crew said they had a truck that was just outside the boundaries of the wilderness area and they could take us the rest of the way down from there. Just as we got there, the horse I was on tossed me off onto the ground, adding insult to injury. I laugh about it now, but when I got in that truck and we started down the road, I felt every bump, stump and rock in it going down that mountain. It was a fun trip up until that point. Even looking back on it, it was still an incredible adventure. Any trip you catch fish on is a good trip! It is just one of those things that can happen in the wilderness and that you have to deal with.

Any trip you catch fish on is a good trip!

Judge Manson retired in late 2005, after the time of this interview.

Lynnea Atlas-Ingebretson

Outdoor Adventure Center Coordinator, Auraria Campus, University of Colorado Denver, Colorado

What I Do in the Outdoors

I moved to Denver from Minnesota two years ago. I came here to go back to school. I work for the University of Colorado Outdoor Adventure Center on the Auraria Campus in Denver. I am the coordinator for the Adventure Leadership Program. I am blessed to be able to put my recreational passion together with my passion for increasing academic success for students of color.

We provide leadership training and diversity retreats in the outdoors where people are put into situations where they have to experience being with people who are different from them, not just talk about it. I really look up to my program director as a white person who is dedicated to the quality that culturally diverse environments bring. I don't know of many college programs that measure their success based on how diverse the groups they take into the outdoors are.

We go to places like the Rocky Mountains, or nearby Utah—as long as it is some kind of natural environment that gives people a chance to get to know one another without all the pretenses and the pressures that society places on us daily about how different we are as individuals.

My husband and I chose to sell our car when we moved to Denver. Part of that is a green decision and part of it is a social decision. The environmental benefit is that it does cut down on greenhouse gas emissions, and the other part is a quality of life benefit. If I get my workout each day by riding my bike to work or walking to work, then I am a much healthier person than I was when I had a car. I also see it as a decision to strengthen community integrity. I really feel that if people are not willing to live where they work, then they should give the job to someone who is willing to live there. I think a lot of that comes from the neighborhood where I grew up in Minneapolis. In that area a lot of companies that do good business hire folks from the neighborhood. Where I come from, making life choices based on quality of life is not weird. It was the culture of the neighborhood, it was the norm.

Best Outdoor Experiences and Favorite Places

My favorite outdoor activity is sea kayaking on Lake Superior back in Minnesota. I was an avid downhill skier in Minnesota, but here in Colorado I am a hard-core snowboarder. If I had no brains at all, I guess I would give up everything in life and just spend all my time in the mountains snowboarding.

I especially love the Boundary Waters Canoe Area of northern Minnesota. It is one of the very few places in this country where you can go and not even see a plane for days, or a telephone pole, let alone another human being, depending on the time of year you are there. There is something very unique about that experience that quiets your spirit enough so that you can look at life with a very fresh set of eyes.

I once spent two weeks during the winter at Adventurous Christians camp in northern Minnesota. Most of that time was spent by myself, supporting the camp, while the owners were on vacation. I would have days when my only company was a group of playful, energetic sled dogs, so I talked to those dogs a lot. I read a lot of books and I also got really, really quiet. For me, being an extrovert, it was a huge challenge to be alone for two weeks. In that time I learned the real beauty of winter in the north-woods—the beauty of a full moon reflecting off the snow at night, or skiing in the early morning over fresh snow.

I especially love the Boundary Waters Canoe Area of northern Minnesota. It is one of the very few places in this country where you can go and not even see a plane for days, or a telephone pole, let alone another human being, depending on the time of year you are there.

Georgia Reid

Birdwatcher
Detroit, Michigan

What I Do in the Outdoors

I am retired—yay! I retired from teaching after 45 years as a modern dance instructor. I taught first at the University of Massachusetts in Amherst. Then in 1971, I came to Detroit to teach at Wayne State University until I retired. I really did not get into birding until I came to Detroit. The campus in Massachusetts was residential, so all of the faculty and students were there. Everybody knew each other and it was a very cozy, nice little setup. When I came to Michigan, I found that it was a commuter campus, so people came in, taught their classes and went home. I began to feel as though I did not really know anyone.

I saw an advertisement for classes through the university center for adult education. The first course I took was "Woody Plants of Michigan." It was fun, but I don't think I really met any new people or made any new friends there. The next term I took "Birds." That was in the mid-1970s, and from then on I was hooked! The course instructor recommended that we join the National Audubon Society. So I joined, and have been a birdwatcher ever since, some 30 years now. It was great—besides the beautiful birds, I met very nice people. I also got to know the area well enough to feel as though I was back home in Massachusetts. With birding, you get to know the areas around where you live pretty well.

I spend as much time as I can trying to become a better birder. I would go birding on the weekends by myself when I was teaching and be so excited about what I had seen that I would walk into class the following Monday and say to my class, "Guess what I saw this weekend?" One day a student walked up to me and said, "My friend told me to take your class because there was this crazy lady who put on this show every Monday morning about the birds she saw over the weekend." So I found out that my students knew me as "the lady who goes birding." It was really nice, actually, because it allowed them to open up and talk about what they had done over the weekend, too. They would say, "I was up north this weekend, and I saw an osprey, and I thought about you." It really made them notice things around them more and pay attention to birds.

During migration in the fall, I go birding every weekend. I drive up to Holiday Beach in southwestern Ontario, Canada, at the mouth of the Detroit River. The bird of prey migration there is incredible.

Best Outdoor Experiences and Favorite Places

I say to everybody, "Go to Alaska!" That, for me, was the trip of a lifetime. It was more spectacular each day. The tour guide would say, "Watch for this bird," and I would be gazing off at the expansive scenery around me. The land just goes on forever, you can see so far and wide. You look out and you realize that those glaciers are many miles away and little bitty me is way over here. It really puts life in perspective.

Many of my long distance bird trips I do with a group from the local nature center. One year we went birding in Alabama, and I remember one afternoon we had a migration movement of tanagers—both scarlet and summer tanagers. It was neat to look up in the trees and see what looked like bright red Christmas tree ornaments flittering around in the branches. I have also birded the Rio Grande Valley of Texas and seen great kiskadees there. I was birding in Alamos, Mexico, and got to see a toucan—you know, the bird from the Fruit Loop cereal commercials. There it was in a tree on the side of the road, where we got great looks at it.

I found out that my students knew me as "the lady who goes birding."

Robert Foxx

Former U.S. Forest Service Wild Lands Firefighter
Fort Collins, Colorado

What I Do in the Outdoors

While I was in college at Oregon State University, I worked as a wild land firefighter for the U.S. Forest Service. I ended that career here in Colorado as an engine foreman with a crew of two. My area to work was the Poudre Canyon just outside of Fort Collins. It was my job to patrol that area, keeping an eye out for wild land fires, and to keep my small crew and that truck ready to go into a fire 24 hours a day, 7 days a week at a moment's notice, if needed.

My Forest Service career began in the town of Oakridge, Oregon. The first year I fought forest fires over summer break from college. In my second year, I stayed with the Forest Service until January, taking a break from school. Then the following year I progressed into the "hot shot crew" in Klamath Falls, Oregon.

I've fought lots of fires of all sizes, from 2- or 3-acre fires to 100,000 acres. Most of the time you had to hike into the fires with a 30- to 40-pound pack on your back. I used to be the lead sorter, so I used to cut down trees and buck them up or break them down and get all the fire out of them. That was a lot of fun. I learned on the job. Up until that time I had never taken a chain saw and cut down a tree in my life, not before I started fighting fires.

I really enjoyed my job. I felt like I was part of a team working for a good cause. I was saving the forest and animals from fire. I also enjoyed all the traveling. Sometimes I would be at a fire for 21 days straight. Then you would go rest up in a nice hotel before going to another fire, sometimes in another state. I remember one time we had just come back from fighting a fire in northern California, and we got back, and on the same day we got another call to go to Idaho and fight another fire. You pack up, get in the plane and off you go. I enjoyed being flown around in helicopters and getting dropped off on fires and working to put them out. It was very exciting. We worked hard and we played hard.

You learn a lot about people and about yourself fighting fires. You work with all kinds of people with different levels of experience, from college kids to seasoned smoke jumpers. You work with people of all races—whites, Native Americans, all with different levels of education. The thing you will find that you all have in common is that you smell like smoke all the time and you are always dirty. You get used to it.

Fatigue sets in all the time. Your muscles get tired and you get blisters on your feet from the heat cooking them in your boots. You say to yourself, "Man, I am not sure how much longer I can do this." Dehydration sets in, with all the sweating from the heat. Once in Alaska I worked 52 hours straight. So it is really kind of a mind-over-matter thing, when you work that long under those kinds of conditions. Everybody needs those kinds of things where they can say to themselves, "I can quit here because this is hard, or I can tough it out and be something." It is a real character builder.

Best Outdoor Experiences and Favorite Places

One of the most amazing experiences I ever had in the outdoors was a mountain biking adventure in Moab, Utah. One of the most beautiful areas I have ever seen. Natural arches of red rock everywhere.

When I was there, I did the 12-mile Slickrock Mountain bike trail. It took me all day to do it. I started at like 7:00 AM and did not get done until 7:00 PM. It is wild! You're coming down over boulders and stuff 20 feet high, coming down on your back tire. It is scary, but it is a natural rush and lots of fun. You're riding your bike along a canyon rim, and you look over the edge, and it is a 50-foot drop into the canyon below. You know if you go over the side, it's all over baby, and send in the life flight choppers!

It was tough, I ain't gonna lie to you; you have to be in good shape. We were there in May, it was like 100 degrees by midmorning or so. But I cannot describe just how beautiful a place it is. There are so many incredible natural rock structures and limestone canyons. It is like God's heaven on earth.

You learn a lot about people and about yourself fighting fires.

Chelsea Griffie

Rock Climber
San Francisco, California

What I Do in the Outdoors

I love rock climbing! Rock climbing rocks! I guess I am addicted to it. I have been doing it for nearly 13 years. I danced for several years during and after college. I also practiced several forms of martial arts around the same time, but once I tried rock climbing, it just fit. I like to keep my body fine-tuned and prepared for whatever challenge I put it up to; that is very important to me. I enjoy rock climbing for its problem-solving puzzles, making me figure things out on my own. There is also the physical element. Best of all, I get to be outside and hang out with really cool people in incredible places that are hard to get to any other way. Pulling all of those elements together, it becomes something that I just can't live without. I jones for it!

Even if I am just bouldering, the only thing that is important to me is the two square feet of rock in front of my face; it really focuses you. You have to figure out a solution to get up that rock, so your mind is just so focused right there in the moment. It is such a welcome break for your brain, that total focus without the day-to-day distractions. I also enjoy trail running and yoga, but those activities are not as mentally engaging for me as climbing.

At the moment I am making my living as an art model and as a server for a catering business in the fine city of San Francisco. My life can be very hectic—my week's activities are constantly changing—so climbing gives my brain a break to focus on just one thing and shut out the stress of daily life.

I led a women-of-color trip for wild women workshops last year. With so many women leading such stressful lives, raising children or just working their butts off out there, nature offers a much-needed break.

Best Outdoor Experiences and Favorite Places

My favorite places to spend time outdoors are Yosemite National Park and Joshua Tree National Monument. I have lots of friends in those areas, and it is nice to visit and climb with them. I also love to climb the Needles area in the southern Sierra Nevada Mountains of California. It is an incredibly beautiful area with just tons and tons of cool climbing to do. I enjoy checking out new areas, too, but some of those classic climbs, like the ones in the Nevadas, I could just do over and over again and never get tired of them. If a climb is considered a "classic climb" by climbers, there is usually a reason for it, and once you climb it you say, "Oh, I see why that is now."

I have had so many memorable experiences outdoors, partly because in climbing you can get to places that are not accessible any other way. For instance, sleeping on a tiny ledge on the face of El Capitan in Yosemite Park, maybe 2,000 feet above the valley floor, is a mind-blowing experience. To get a visual of what that is like, imagine climbing on the outside of a 3,000-foot skyscraper, and about two-thirds of the way up you have to sleep overnight on a window ledge until the next morning. That is something at one time I thought I would have never been able to do. People ask me, "How can you relax? How can you sleep?" I mean, when evening comes and you are still at least 1,000 feet from the summit on a 3,000-foot vertical granite rock face, you have to sleep somewhere. You are happy to find a place you can sit still for several hours and feel the breeze go by, or watch the sunset or the moonrise. It is just good to be able to rest and collect your thoughts after a long day of climbing.

I love rock climbing! Rock climbing rocks! I guess I am addicted to it.

Mamie Parker

Assistant Director of Fisheries and Habitat Conservation, U.S. Fish and Wildlife Service
Washington, D.C.

What I Do in the Outdoors

One day when I was in college, I had gone fishing and returned to discover staff from the university wanted to talk to me. Hannibal Bolton, who worked for the U.S. Fish and Wildlife Service, was recruiting minorities to come and work for the organization. He was like a used car salesman, and he sold me on the Service idea. By the time he was done talking I was like, "Of course I will take the position. That sounds like the fun place to be." He led me to believe it was somewhere in Arkansas, but I later discovered that the job was in Wisconsin. When I called him up and asked, "Isn't it very cold in Wisconsin?" He said, "Yes, it can be." And like a used car salesman, he told me, "Let me see what I can do." He called me back and said, "I tell you what, we will throw in some clothes for you." Those clothes turned out to be a Service uniform, and everybody who worked for them got them free. Just like a car salesman, I did not see him again after that for many years, but now he works for me. He was really passionate about the Service, and he really pulled me into it.

I really enjoyed working and fishing in Wisconsin and Minnesota. The one commonality of living in southwestern Wisconsin and the Deep South was the great Mississippi River. Whenever I got homesick, I would just go down to the river and that was always a good feeling. I had a lot of Fish and Wildlife jobs in the upper Midwest. In Wisconsin I got introduced to ice fishing and enjoyed that a lot. In Missouri I learned some different things about the outdoors and got involved in what we now call the Partners for Fish and Wildlife program. That program involved working with landowners to get them to convert farms to land that would protect or increase wildlife populations. So I got introduced to pheasant, quail and turkey hunting, and really enjoyed working with farmers there.

My job title now is Assistant Director of Fisheries and Habitat Conversation. The facilities include 70 National Fish Hatcheries, 64 Fishery Resource Offices, 9 Fish Health Centers, 7 Fish Technology Centers and over 50 Ecological Services Offices. We also have one genetic lab and one historic hatchery. I set guidance and policy for about 2,400 employees throughout the nation. There is an enormous sense of responsibility and duty that comes with my job, and I take it very seriously. Being the first African American female in many of the job titles I have held with the Service is not something I want to brag about but it does mean I have a lot of people looking up to me, and that is what motivates me to want to do more and be the best I can at what I do. Ms. Mary Bethune, an African American woman of many accomplishments in education for minority women in the early 1900s, said, "Lift as we climb," meaning it is up to those who succeed in life to bring others up with them. So that when we turn around and look in life, we see there are others following in our footsteps.

Best Outdoor Experiences and Favorite Places

In our family, fishing was more than about recreation, but also about putting protein on our dinner table. For me, fishing on those riverbanks with my mother became a place to learn life lessons. I remember sitting on the banks of Lake Enterprise in southeast Arkansas with my mama one day. That was the first time we ever went fishing together. I picked up a Coca Cola bottle from the mud and said, "Look, Mama, I can read!" She said, "What does it say, baby?" I told her, "No deposit, no return," and she said, "There is a life lesson in there. You have to make investments in yourself and others in order to get something back in life." I must have caught bass and bluegill that day but it is not the fish I remember the most; it is the life lessons I learned that stand out the most in my mind from that special day with my mama. I have never forgotten them.

Whenever I got homesick, I would just go down to the river and that was always a good feeling.

Hank Williams Jr.

Big Game Hunter and Black Cowboy
Rush City, Minnesota

What I Do in the Outdoors

Hunting is the big thing for me, and big game is the most fun. That means elk, deer, bear—those kinds of animals. Discovering new areas and all the research involved in that, and talking with local hunters all add an element of excitement for me. Being outside in different landscapes is also very exciting to me. By trade I am an electronic technician. I work in the semiconductor business, where we maintain equipment and do repairs.

Horses are another big thing of mine in the off-season. I enjoy roping and riding. I enjoy working with these animals. They are athletes, but on a different level. They will require you to step up your physical abilities just to be able to work with them. So when you work with horses in a competition, you are not only competing against other riders, but against their horses as well. I just bought 32 acres of land here in northern Minnesota and I am building a new house, horse stables and a riding and roping arena. All of my roping friends are white who live in my community. I know there are other black ropers around the country, but we are kind of scattered. I would like to help others learn about the sport in the future. I already have a young black student who is the daughter of my best friend. I started out showing her older brother how to throw a rope, and when she saw it she became interested. It turned out he never really took a liking to it and gave it up, but she really wanted to learn more, so I work with her on it, and she is coming along real nice.

Camping is another thing I enjoy, along with fishing and anything that puts me in the outdoors that requires my physical and mental attention.

Best Outdoor Experiences and Favorite Places

One outing that stands out in my mind involved bear hunting. I was up in my bear stand one fall, and after a while I saw a fairly large bear, maybe 400 or so pounds, appear at the edge of the woods. The bear did not come in too close. I had put out bait, but it just stayed on the perimeter. I thought to myself, "Something is different here. This bear is acting a bit unusual." After a while it came in closer to the bait. It still did not come all the way in, but it did get a little closer. Then after a while, one little bear cub appears and pops out of the woods, then another, until there were four cubs!

Now most sows will have three in a year, but she had four. So I watched them eat the bait and she just hung back and kept an eye out. The four little cubs came in and filled their little bellies so much they were dragging on the ground. Anytime there was a little noise in the woods, it would send them running up a tree until the sow would give them the OK to come back down and feed.

Needless to say, I never shot her. I watched her and her cubs for two years. They sure were fun to watch. I would just take pictures of them running around wrestling with each other. Then in the third season she did not come back anymore. I figured now her cubs were two or three years old, so they were on their own and she had probably moved on to a different territory.

Hunting is the big thing for me, and big game is the most fun. That means elk, deer, bear—those kinds of animals.

Judie Johnson

Executive Director, Gunflint Trail Association
Grand Marais, Minnesota

What I Do in the Outdoors

I am the Executive Director of the Gunflint Trail Association in northeastern Minnesota. The Gunflint is a vacation destination for people from around the region and the world. The 57-mile paved highway goes north out of Grand Marais, Minnesota, through some of the most beautiful wilderness area you may ever see, and turns west, ending on Saganaga Lake near the Canadian border. People visit the trail to access the Boundary Waters Canoe Area. There is so much to do off the Gunflint at anytime of the year, including fishing, camping, and hiking and skiing in the winter. You can watch wildlife at all times of the year. Moose, bears, wolves, deer and a host of other cool animals make the area their home. The best part about my job is telling tourists how to have fun in a place that I love.

By most people's standards, Grand Marais would seem very remote. Most of what we do here is outdoors. Closest movie theater or shopping mall is 75 miles away. I tell people, "There is Lake Superior, it's right there in front of you. It is the largest freshwater lake in the world, and you can't find anything to do?"

I actually bought land here, knowing that some day I wanted to move here. I remembered my mother telling me that when I was 10 years old I returned from a summer camp in Wisconsin and announced that I was moving to the woods when I grew up. So when I moved up here to Grand Marais, it was no shock to her. I am pretty sure I am the only black woman living in the whole town. People asked my mom, "What is wrong with Judie?" And she told them, "Judie told me she was moving to the woods a long time ago, and now she has finally done it."

Best Outdoor Experiences and Favorite Places

My favorite outdoor activity depends on the time of year. I love skiing—doesn't matter if it's cross-country, downhill or telemark. I enjoy riding my mountain bike, rock climbing, trail running, swimming in fresh water, canoeing and kayaking. My favorite activity is always whatever I am doing at that moment until I can do the next thing. It's fun to combine activities like canoeing and rock climbing in the same day on one trip! Those are great days because you put so much of yourself into them and so you sleep like a zombie at night.

Traveling abroad gave me a unique perspective on how people in other cultures live. When I was in China and Peru, the animals that were found in the street markets were an eye opener to me. Seeing things that you knew were endangered species for sale really shocked me. OK, you know poaching and other illegal acts happen intellectually, but seeing it right at arm's length is very different.

The lost city of Machu Picchu on the Inca Trail in Peru is a very spiritual and sacred place. There is a place at Machu Picchu where the sun comes through the stone perfectly during the spring equinox. There is a mountain above Machu Picchu called Jaguar, and when you climb up there you understand everything. I understood why Machu Picchu was built there. And I had studied the Great Wall of China for quite a while in college, so when I stood on it I understood completely why they built it. You could see forever.

Traveling abroad gave me a unique perspective on how people in other cultures live.

Marshall Reese

Assistant Park Manager and Ranger, Franklin County Metropolitan Park System
Columbus, Ohio

What I Do in the Outdoors

I got into nature in an odd kind of way. I can remember it plain as day. I was sitting with my folks just after my sister had graduated from college, and I had just graduated from high school. We were sitting there talking about what I was going to do and if I wanted to continue into college. They said, "Son, you are going to have to do something. What about forestry?"

I eventually decided on the military, and I served down at Fort Campbell, in Kentucky, which was a short distance from where my entire family was from. I loved the Army, refueling helicopters and stuff, and just enjoyed being out-of-doors.

I stayed in the Army for five years. When I got out, I realized I really enjoyed the outdoors, so I went and worked with Big Brothers and Big Sisters at their summer camps, and had lots of fun showing kids all the cool stuff along hikes, helping inner city kids experience the outdoors. That was a joy for me, because many of those city kids had never seen a lot of nature and I could show them and say, "Check it out!" And they were happy to learn all the cool outdoor stuff I showed them. I thought maybe, just maybe, a kid would enjoy it enough to think, "Hey, maybe this is what I want to do for a career—be outdoors."

After that I really wanted to get back into law enforcement, so I did corrections first, and enjoyed that. Then this job came along. It was the perfect setting, because I love being outdoors. As a full-time ranger in law enforcement, I had to go to a police academy and graduate. I graduated third in my class. I was one of the class officers. Unfortunately, I did not have the formal training most of my colleagues have; I did not go to school for forestry, which would have put me on par with most of the other students in my graduating class.

My official title here is Assistant Park Manager with the Franklin County Metro Park Systems of Columbus, Ohio, serving at Sharon Woods Metro Park. My job here is the same as the manager's job. If the manager is not here, I run the park. If he is here and is too busy doing paperwork, I run the park. I can also decide to come in today and put on a maintenance uniform and go brush some trails or mow and repair something.

We do have weapons, but not the firearm type. I get my point across and get the rules enforced just fine without them. I have had to arrest people in the park. Sometimes people in the park don't understand that our rangers here are full-time certified peace officers. We have the same authority to enforce the laws in the same way as state officers, such as highway patrol and local township and city police.

Best Outdoor Experiences and Favorite Places

I tell you, I ain't even gonna lie, my favorite outdoor activity is golf. It's all about golf! It is the best of both worlds; you got the sports part, you are getting some exercise, and then there is the mental aspect. We were down in Myrtle Beach, my wife and I and another couple, and we were golfing, and I saw some of the most beautiful woodpeckers and warblers and a different finch that I had never seen in Ohio. Really, where else would you see that, unless you go birding in some type of sanctuary? Golf rolls it all up into one great package. I mean, some places I have been, you stand there on those tees and you have forest on one side and ocean on the other, and you say, "Man, God did a great job. This is beautiful. He gave man the knowledge to create such a serene scene in which to calm people so they can hit this shot."

Golf rolls it all up into one great package. I mean, some places I have been, you stand there on those tees and you have forest on one side and ocean on the other, and you say, "Man, God did a great job. This is beautiful."

Phadrea Ponds

Wildlife Biologist, U.S. Geological Survey
Fort Collins, Colorado

What I Do in the Outdoors

I am a wildlife biologist. I specialize in human dimension research. If people live in an area or are recreating in the area, I look at how their activities affect the land or wildlife habitat. I study data collected by surveying the public or holding public meetings and focus groups.

A lot of people think they can use the land any way they want because it is public land. We try to let them know that yes, they can use the land because it is their natural heritage, but recognize that the wildlife uses the land as well. We teach them about how to respect it.

I did not grow up wanting be a wildlife biologist. It was one of those things—doors started opening for me, and I just kind of went through them. It was serendipitous that I got into this field. I am certain that it was because people took an interest in me and helped me to understand what my potential was.

In college, I wanted to know more. I was more intrigued by the learning element of natural resources versus the actual physical element of it, and then once I learned it, I wanted to see it and touch it. Once I learned about the anatomy and physiology of a particular bird, I really wanted to find that bird. For me that was completing the circle. Once I learned about a plant species, I wanted to go out and find that plant.

Best Outdoor Experiences and Favorite Places

I love bird watching. I was real good at one time—very good. I knew the bird calls and everything. Now I am a bit rusty. I still have a life list; I know what I have and have not seen. Every opportunity I get, I am listening and watching for birds. My favorite bird is the painted bunting.

The mountains are special to me. The mountain air is very cool—I can think. I can hear myself think, I can sort through things that I can't in the confines of brick buildings. The mountains are so huge, I think they can take every thing I have to release. I can't release it in the city environment, because it will bounce back, for lack of a better explanation. But in the mountains it will be absorbed and I can just let it go and leave it there.

My first enjoyable outdoor experience was during my days in college at Grambling, and after that it was on dates with my husband before we were married. One day he said, "Do you want to go camping?" I said, "Yeah," but the truth was I had never been camping before. That was when we were at Oregon State. I could not let him think I did not know how to camp. So I played this game right up to the last second. I had taken all of this stuff. I had a cooler full of food and candles for a candlelight dinner. And he was like, "Where are you going with all of this stuff?" He said, "No, dear, that is not what we are going to do." I said, "Well, what are we going to do?" So we hiked in and he opened up some trees, and then we walked in farther and he opened up some more trees, and then he said, "I guess we will stop here." I thought, "This is not a campground. This is just a patch in the middle of forest." We made a fire, we put the tent up and slept on the ground. After a few more camping trips I got used to it and began to enjoy it.

Being a wife and a great mother has been a life goal for me. The way that I experience things now is through experiences with my family; they are no longer just personal experiences. My husband and I can take the time to go out and go camping, or we could spend a day in Utah's Canyonlands National Park over a weekend and do those types of things together. We are looking forward to doing those kinds of things with the girls.

Every opportunity I get, I am listening and watching for birds. My favorite bird is the painted bunting.

Alex Johnson

Oregon State University Graduate
Portland, Oregon

What I Do in the Outdoors

I recently graduated from Oregon State University. I actually wrote my own degree program, which is a Bachelor of Science in natural resources, with an emphasis on cultural dimensions and recreation. I really want to work in some sort of park facility administration. I am looking at a master's program in public administration.

I spent half of my life in Denver and half of my life up here in Portland, Oregon. I spent most of my time growing up in an inner city environment. Once I moved to Portland, I spent a lot of time growing up in the natural areas around our neighborhood.

My oldest brother was the one who actually got me connected with the Forest Park Ivy Removal Project. It is a joint venture between Portland Parks and Recreation and the Friends of Forest Park that employs a diverse group of youth crews to remove invasive ivy plants that are choking off native trees and other native plants. We travel together through the forest, using a number of tools to get the job done, including machetes, hatchets and saws. I first started out as a youth crew member with the project in 1996, a year after my brother had worked for the project. I worked my way from a youth crew member during the summers, all the way up working year-round as a crew leader and summer program supervisor. You could say I grew up with the project. When I started with the project it was probably only in its third or fourth year of existence, so it was real fresh, and a lot of the youth I grew up with were in the project. They were really a diverse group. That is how I first became really interested in nature and the outdoors.

I would say to youth of color, "Do not blindly follow the paths mapped out for you," to almost quote the book *Black Boy* by famous black author Richard Wright. You play a sport because you think that is the only thing you can do to advance yourself in this world. I did not want to go down that road. I picked myself up academically in resource issues, and because of my background, a door opened for me.

Just by my association with the Forest Park landscape, I realized there is more that I can do with my life than I had dreamed of before. I realized the way people interact with the land is really important. My experience working with the youth crews here in Forest Park has been the turning point in my life, the thing that changed me forever. Now I have a natural resources degree because I worked here as a youth crew member and leader.

I have also been involved in hip-hop music all of my adult life. My hip-hop pseudo name is "Sun Kissed." They nicknamed me that because I always want to work towards something positive, creating music that makes people feel good but still has intellectual content. Habitat restoration, in the case of my current solo project, is a metaphor for how music had been devoid of the things I needed to make it work for me. That is completely related to my natural resources experience, because that is what I had been doing the whole time, restoring habitat. We need to restore the habitat of hip-hop and what it began as—a voice of the people for political issues for real positive messages. I hope to be able to reach people about the issues I care about with my music, such as natural resources preservation.

Best Outdoor Experiences and Favorite Places

I have a favorite place I go camping near Mount Hood here in Oregon. It is called Trillium Lake and I have had experiences there with my family that will stay with me the rest of my life. It feels unreal to see all the trilliums growing there along this lake that is shaped like a trillium. Getting out in nature helps you appreciate life and appreciate that every moment can be picture perfect and to enjoy every moment of your life to its fullest.

Getting out in nature helps you appreciate life.

Brian Gilbert

Backcountry Ranger
Rocky Mountain National Park, Colorado

What I Do in the Outdoors

Currently I am a backcountry ranger with the National Park Service at Rocky Mountain National Park in Colorado. My job entails issuing permits to any visitor coming into the national park for a backcountry outing. On a typical day I issue on average about 20 to 30 backcountry permits, which allow visitors to camp or travel up to seven days or nights within the remote backcountry regions of the park during the summer.

When I am out there in the backcountry as a ranger on my official hike day, I have people coming up to me asking questions. I find myself perhaps overpreparing for these encounters, knowing that eventually someone will ask me a question, and when they do I will have to answer the question knowledgeably and factually. I read ravenously. I have books and magazines around here everywhere. I am constantly reading. The more I know, the more I can help visitors to the backcountry better enjoy their experience.

Best Outdoor Experiences and Favorite Places

One year, when I was 14, my aunt packed us all up and took us to Yellowstone National Park in her RV. We spent about 24 days out there. We would day hike in the park and meet some of the rangers, and they would give us talks about the park. I had a blast! I had never seen anything like that in my life. I was used to small houses, shootings on street corners, you know, the drug deals you would see on the street corners almost daily. Then getting into places like the national parks where you don't see any of that, it kind of just throws you for a loop. You look down a canyon and 500 feet below you there's running water. You ask, "How did it get that way?" When a ranger explains to you about how shifts and geological cracks and water erosion work together to form the canyon—it really amazed me. Being the bookworm that I am, I jumped into the subject matter and was hooked on it. It was then that I began to realize I had to broaden my horizons; I had to get away from the city.

I am a city slicker for sure. Until this job I had never done any serious backcountry hiking in my entire life. It was an absolutely wonderful experience. I have never tent camped before, so I hope to do that many times before I leave the park this summer. I can't say enough that it is such an awesome, spiritual experience when I get out into the backcountry. I drove up the top of Trail Ridge Road here in Rocky Mountain National Park, which peaks at about 13,500 feet. I had never been up that high in a car before. I was so overcome by what I was able to see with my eyes that I have to admit I cried a bit. I was like, "Man, there is no way to describe this." It was just amazing.

If anything, being outdoors gives me the opportunity to learn more about myself. When you get out there away from people, where you do not hear anything except maybe water in a river or the wind whistling through the trees, you develop such clarity in your thoughts. Anything you are worried about or obsessing over becomes clearer in your mind—you become much more proactive and you come up with solutions where you thought there were none.

I can't say enough that it is such an awesome, spiritual experience when I get out into the backcountry.

Frank & Audrey Peterman

Conservationists
Atlanta, Georgia

What I Do in the Outdoors

AUDREY: As an immigrant from Jamaica, I had never heard of the National Park System even though I had lived in the U.S. for 15 years prior to our marriage. Of course, I had heard of the Grand Canyon and Yellowstone, but they were nowhere I thought I would ever go. When Frank and I got married in 1992, he shared this desire he had for us to travel around the country and discover America through the national parks. My God, that started us on the greatest adventure of our lives and ultimately took us to where we are today, as people deeply involved in conservation. I would suggest that every breath we breathe that is not given to each other, or our children, or our friends is really given to the conservation of the natural world.

FRANK: Presently, I am Regional Public and Political Awareness Director for the Wilderness Society for the East Coast, which is from the state of Maine to Florida. I try to figure out ways to actually build a constituency in the African American community to support wilderness conservation and land protection. That is job number one! We have begun to work with historically black colleges and universities, which are the land grant colleges that were set up right after slavery ended for African Americans. I also work a great deal with the Congressional Black Caucus. We are trying to show the African

American community the connections between their health and welfare and the protection of these very special wild places.

AUDREY: I manage our website, earthwiseproductionsinc.com, and I publish the newsletter "Pick up & GO!" It is a bimonthly newsletter that focuses on the environment and travel to the national parks. The idea being that if we show people of color the existence of these beautiful places first of all, then we show them that there is black history in these places that is not widely known, we might get their attention. We also show them the connection to the larger environmental debate and how it affects their lives, both in terms of the conservation of green spaces and in terms of the pollution in the cities, and how their actions can affect both of those issues.

Some of the most interesting and enjoyable things we have done include lobbying Congress to help get the Selma to Montgomery National Historic Trail in Alabama. We helped to get that legislation passed. We helped to get legislation passed for the National Underground Railroad Network to Freedom. When you go out and visit the national parks, and you show somebody, and you say, "Hey, this belongs to you. Your tax dollars pay for this. It is part of your natural heritage." Then you tell them about their ancestors who were there as enslaved Africans, who found their freedom going through the Everglades on to places like the Bahamas, etc., or that Colonel Charles Young and the Buffalo Soldiers were the ones who protected the giant sequoias in 1903—then African Americans begin to see themselves reflected in the fabric of the country in ways that the history books don't show them.

Best Outdoor Experiences and Favorite Places

AUDREY: Frank and I saved up our money for a year, and we bought some camping and hiking equipment. We took off from Florida and drove all the way up the East Coast to Acadia National Park. Camped out for the first time in our lives right there in the park. Then we drove up Cadillac Mountain, where we were above the clouds, and the scenery was so beautiful that it was almost heart stopping. Then we drove across the middle of the country to visit Yellowstone National Park, and to our amazement we discovered it was not just about one geyser. We learned that, in fact, this was world's largest concentration of geysers, right there in Yellowstone. From there we drove to the Grand Canyon, which cannot be described. It must be experienced to be believed. Then we continued on to Olympic National Park, where we were able to experience the rain forest on one side of the road, and wade out into the ocean and actually touch sea creatures and starfish on the other side of the road. It was just an incredible, amazing, wonderful experience. Then we drove to the Petrified National Forest, where we saw trees that had turned to stone over millions of years, and they were glowing like 40-ton jewels. The year was 1995, and we traveled from August to October. We were completely captivated, and we fell madly in love with the national park system.

Then we drove to the Petrified National Forest, where we saw trees that had turned to stone over millions of years, and they were glowing like 40-ton jewels.

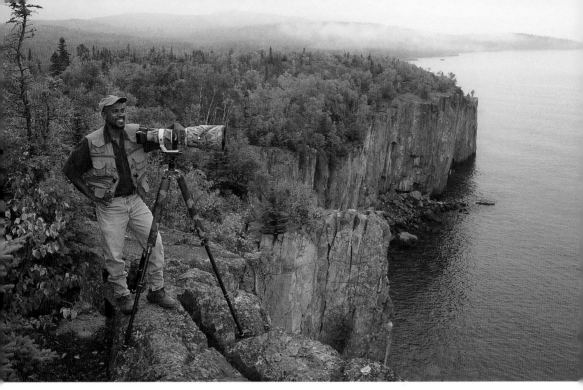

Dudley Edmondson

Professional Nature Photographer and Writer
Duluth, Minnesota

What I Do in the Outdoors

I moved north to Minnesota in 1989, looking for a fresh start and a career as a nature photographer. I did not really have a plan for how I was going to go about it, just the desire to make it happen. When I think back on it today, I think one of the reasons it worked was that it never occurred to me that I couldn't do it. I followed leads, read books and magazines on nature photography and just stuck with it.

All my efforts paid off when I got a call from a local author who was looking for photos of birds for a field guide he was writing. His guide really sold well and he began branching out into regional, then national guides covering common flora and fauna. We started traveling nationwide, shooting on location from Alaska to Florida and every state in between. We became a serious photographic duo and always got publication-quality images of the species we were after.

We would build our own outdoor studio on site when needed. We developed a way to photograph reptiles, amphibians and small mammals without harming them or removing them from their habitats. We'd set up a small enclosure around the animal and maybe add some leaves, a rock or a piece of log. Once we got the shots we wanted, we took down the enclosure and returned the natural elements to their original places. Sometimes these studio setups would require a few extra bits and pieces, so we both carried spring clamps, duct tape, wood scraps and cordless power tools in our SUVs, just in case. Some of the shots we got of elusive species were incredible.

I found that photographing wildlife takes a lot of patience. I would say it might be the single most important component of the job. You have to study their behavior and determine the best time and location to get a publication-quality image. Learning predictable patterns like migration routes or nesting behavior gives you a slight, but large enough advantage to achieve your objective.

Today I am slowly remolding myself to become an outdoor adventure photographer, chasing down mountain climbers, kayakers and extreme sport enthusiasts of all types. Specifically, I've been looking for African Americans and other people of color in these activities, in an effort to create images that could change the way people of color see themselves and maybe, in the process, also change the way America sees them. In this country, African Americans and other minorities are often seen or referred to as a group, rather than as individuals, and that bugs me. I say, "See the individuals—be an individual!"

Best Outdoor Experiences and Favorite Places

One of my more memorable experiences in the outdoors was the first time I experienced complete and utter silence in the outdoors. I was on my first trip to South Dakota, a solo trip to visit Badlands National Park, the first national park I ever visited in the United States. It was a completely different environment than I had ever been in before. I set out across the flatlands, heading towards the base of a set of buttes about a mile away. Once there, I stopped, looked around and listened intently. The only sound I heard was the muffled thump of my beating heart—that was it.

I was outside in broad daylight, sun shining, midday, but in total silence. I looked around again. This time I stuck my fingers in my ears. When I removed them, I could not tell the difference. I thought to myself, "This cannot be possible. No sound at all?" No cars, no planes, no people, no television or radio, no animals, no wind, just complete and utter silence. I was nearly in shock. I just laughed kind of nervously and said, "Wow," in a low, whispering tone. The word barely fell off my bottom lip.

I stood there for several minutes, absorbing the quiet, being careful not to move my feet in the dry soil, as I knew it would break the silence. It may have also been one of the first times I really understood and felt the restorative powers of nature. I eventually set up my camera and took some photographs of the buttes before me. Viewing that image today still brings me back to that place, where for a moment it seemed as if time stood still.

I've been looking for African Americans and other people of color in these activities, in an effort to create images that could change the way people of color see themselves and maybe, in the process, also change the way America sees them.

About the Author/Biography

Dudley Edmondson has spent the last 15 years photographing nature and wildlife subjects around the country for natural history publications in the United States and Europe. Dudley proudly carries on a family tradition started by his great-grandfather Monteith Vance, a portrait photographer issued a photography license by the state of North Carolina in 1919.

Four years ago he began work on *Black & Brown Faces in America's Wild Places* in an attempt to find other African Americans around the nation who shared his love for nature and the outdoors. He found several, many of whom he now considers friends. Not until 2005 had he ever been on an outdoor adventure entirely in the company of African Americans; it was a life-affirming experience that he will never forget.

"Nature without question is for everyone. It knows no race, creed or gender and is cheaper that any therapist you could ever hire."

Visit Dudley's website at www.raptorworks.com or contact him at dudley@raptorworks.com